Anne Frank *and the* Remembering Tree

by Sandy Eisenberg Sasso

illustrated by Erika Steiskal

Published by
The Children's Museum of Indianapolis,
3000 North Meridian St., Indianapolis, IN 46208, **www.childrensmuseum.org**

and

Skinner House Books, an imprint of the Unitarian Universalist Association,
24 Farnsworth St., Boston, MA 02210, **www.skinnerhouse.org**

Printed in the United States

ISBN: 978-1-55896-738-0

Sasso photo by Rich Clark Photography
Steiskal photo by Scott Eklund, Red Box Photography
6 5 4 3 2 1
17 16 15

Library of Congress Cataloging-in-Publication Data

Sasso, Sandy Eisenberg, author.
  Anne Frank and the remembering tree / by Sandy Eisenberg Sasso ; illustrated by Erika Steiskal.
    pages cm
  ISBN 978-1-55896-738-0 (hardcover : alk. paper) 1. Frank, Anne, 1929-1945—
Juvenile literature. 2. Jewish children in the Holocaust—Netherlands—Amsterdam—
Biography—Juvenile literature. 3. Jews—Netherlands—Amsterdam—Biography—
Juvenile literature. I. Steiskal, Erika, 1984- illustrator. II. Title.
  DS135.N6F73557 2014
  940.53'18092—dc23
  [B]
                          2014004879

To my friends
Mike Bornstein, who was liberated from Auschwitz at five years of age,
and his wife, Judy.
Together they planted new saplings that blossomed into a family
of four children and eleven grandchildren.

The author, The Children's Museum of Indianapolis, and Skinner House Books
are grateful to Lori Efroymson and the Efroymson Family Foundation
for their generous support, which made this book possible,
and for their vision of a better future for all our children.

I was planted in the heart of Amsterdam, a city of skinny streets, of canals and bridges.

I could see the tall bell tower
of the church in the distance. I
looked over the buildings and watched
people on their bicycles. Children in the
houses around the courtyard picked my chestnuts
when they fell to the ground in autumn.

"That's a horse chestnut tree, and the fruit is not for eating,"
mothers told their sons and daughters as they collected the green
spiky shells with the dark nuts inside. I liked it when children
used my chestnuts to make puppets and play games. I loved to
hear them laugh. Smiles and laughter were like the sunshine and
rain that helped me to grow.

One day, people along the canals of Amsterdam
stopped smiling and laughing. There were
German soldiers everywhere. I heard people call
them Nazis. The Nazis hated anyone who was
not like them, especially the Jewish people. They
wanted to get rid of all the Jews in Europe.
I didn't understand why anyone would want
to do this. But I was just a tree.

I did not like the sound of black boots
marching on the cobblestone sidewalks,
the sirens, or the shouting in the streets.
Why wouldn't people who liked different
kinds of trees and flowers also like many
different kinds of people? It made no
sense to me. But I was just a tree.

I had always looked into the windows of the houses
around the courtyard. In most windows, I saw people
working and children playing. When the soldiers came,
people began covering their windows, so I couldn't see
inside anymore.

But the tiny attic window of the narrow brick house
behind Otto Frank's business offices had no window
shade. For a long time, the rooms were empty. Then one
day, Otto's whole family came to live there. They called
their new home the Secret Annex.

The Franks were Jews. They were hiding from the Nazis. Before long, four other people joined them. I couldn't understand how eight people could live in such a small place. But I was just a tree.

At certain times, all eight people would gather around a small radio to listen to news about the war.

I liked to watch Otto's daughters. The older one was called Margot. She was sixteen years old. Anne was thirteen. Both sisters liked to write in their diaries about what was happening and how they were feeling. Margot was very quiet and shy; she never let me see what she wrote.

Anne would climb up to the attic, sit on a
wooden crate, and listen to the church bells
chime. Because I looked into the window, I
could see Anne writing in her red and white
checked diary. She was writing about me!

She wrote that as long as she could see blue
sky and clouds and me, she could be happy.
Her words made me happy too.

Anne described the ways I changed through
the seasons—my white flowers in spring,
my dark green leaves in summer, and my
chestnuts in autumn. She even marveled
at how the rain froze like diamonds on my
winter branches.

"Anne and Margot, come out and play!"
I called to them through the attic window.
"Come sit in my shade, pick my chestnuts,
and play games." But even though I was just
a tree, I knew they couldn't. They were afraid.

Sometimes Anne and Margot would climb up to the attic to get away from all the adults. They would read books and look up at the attic window to see the rooftops of all the houses and the bell tower of the church. Often they laughed.

"Why are you laughing?" I would ask. "What are you thinking?" Anne and Margot answered by writing to me in their diaries. Being a tree doesn't stop you from feeling what people feel. And when someone loves you, you know it and it helps you grow.

Anne and Margot kept growing too. Sometimes at twilight they would come to the attic and speak softly to each other. I wanted to hear what they were saying. But even though I was just a tree, I understood that their words were just between them.

Then one day in late summer, the Franks heard
heavy footsteps and a group of Nazi soldiers burst
into the room. They made everyone in the Secret
Annex go with them, including Anne and Margot.

"Don't leave," I called after them. "Come outside. I will hide you in my branches." But Anne and Margot couldn't hear. The shouting of the soldiers was too loud.

For many days and nights, I kept looking in the window, hoping that Anne and Margot would return. But they never did.

Several years later, Otto Frank came back alone. "Where are Anne and Margot?" I asked. But only children can understand the language of trees.

Then a good friend, who had helped the Franks while they lived in the Secret Annex, gave Otto Anne's diary. "I saved it hoping someone would come back," she said. Otto held the red and white checkered book in his hands. "And Margot's?" he asked. She lowered her eyes, "We never found it."

Years passed—winters, springs, summers, and falls. I missed Anne and Margot and their dreams. Margot had wanted to be a nurse to help bring new babies into the world. Anne wanted to be a writer.

Before long, people were reading Anne's diary and coming to look at me. They came to see the tree she saw from the window of the Secret Annex.

I was just a tree, but Anne had made me famous. I was glad that people remembered Anne and Margot when they saw me.

Even though people cared for me, eventually I became
sick. They put metal beams around me so I could stand.
Then one day a big storm wind blew so hard that I broke.
I was 170 years old.

I couldn't stand any more. People took pieces from my
branches to grow into new little trees, called saplings.
One day those saplings will be 100 feet tall.

I was just one tree, but now I am many. People planted my saplings in places around the world as reminders of what happened to Anne and Margot and what hatred can do.

They planted them so that everywhere adults and children will recall the hope and promise of two young girls who loved a tree and the tree who remembered them.

FOR FAMILIES AND SCHOOLS

The saplings from the chestnut tree behind the Secret Annex are planted or slated to be planted in eleven places around the United States at the time of this book's printing. Each place is a reminder of the importance of tolerance and the continuing search for justice and peace.

Boston Common in Boston, Massachusetts
Boston has a rich history of celebrating democracy.

Little Rock High School, Little Rock, Arkansas
Nine African-American students integrated the all white high school in 1957. They ultimately succeeded in moving the country closer to desegregation.

William J. Clinton Presidential Library
The sapling stands as a reminder of Arkansas' journey toward tolerance.

Sonoma State University, California
The sapling is being planted at the Rena and Arthur Sahm Holocaust and Memorial Grove.

Idaho Human Rights Center, Boise, Idaho
An Anne Frank statue and memorial park there encourage visitors to speak out against injustice.

The Children's Museum, Indianapolis, Indiana
The museum includes a replica of Anne's Secret Annex as part of The Power of Children: Making A Difference, which includes exhibits about Ruby Bridges and Ryan White.

Holocaust Memorial Center, Farmington Hills, Michigan
This is America's first free-standing Holocaust museum.

Liberty Park, New York, New York
The sapling is planted in remembrance of 9/11 near the National September 11 Memorial and Museum.

Southern Cayuga Central School District, Aurora, New York
The sapling serves as a reminder of how young voices can make a difference in bringing about greater tolerance. This region has been at the forefront of the Civil Rights movement and the quest for greater social justice.

Washington State Holocaust Education Resource Center, Seattle, Washington
The sapling serves as a symbol of the region's common vision for peace, justice, and mutual respect.

U.S. Capitol, Washington, D.C.
Several pieces of tolerance legislation became law here.

Saplings from the chestnut tree have also been planted in 32 countries around the world, including Argentina, Amsterdam, Canada, England, Israel, Japan, Madrid, and Paris.